PRAISE FOR 'NON-PRACTICING CULTIST'

"...has a hard edge that moves quickly to the final scene, it wastes no time with junk we don't need."
– Strange Brew (via Amazon)

"...exciting, creepy, and bloody. It's definitely recommended for fans of horror."
- ReadingReviewingRecommending (via Amazon)

"Another masterpiece of thought, mystery and yes, wanting more!!"
– Brad Scott (via Goodreads)

"[There is] a thrilling unpredictability to *Non-Practicing Cultist*."
– Justin Montgomery (via Horror Oasis)

DEMAIN PUBLISHING

Short Sharp Shocks!

Book 0: Dirty Paws - Dean M. Drinkel
Book 1: Patient K - Barbie Wilde
Book 2: The Stranger & The Ribbon – Tim Dry
Book 3: Asylum Of Shadows – Stephanie Ellis
Book 4: Monster Beach – Ritchie Valentine Smith
Book 5: Beasties & Other Stories – Martin Richmond
Book 6: Every Moon Atrocious – Emile-Louis Tomas Jouvet
Book 7: A Monster Met – Liz Tuckwell
Book 8: The Intruders & Other Stories – Jason D. Brawn
Book 9: The Other – David Youngquist
Book 10: Symphony Of Blood – Leah Crowley
Book 11: Shattered – Anthony Watson
Book 12: The Devil's Portion – Benedict J. Jones
Book 13: Cinders Of A Blind Man Who Could See – Kev Harrison
Book 14: Dulce Et Decorum Est – Dan Howarth
Book 15: Blood, Bears & Dolls – Allison Weir
Book 16: The Forest Is Hungry – Chris Stanley
Book 17: The Town That Feared Dusk – Calvin Demmer
Book 18: Night Of The Rider – Alyson Faye
Book 19: Isidora's Pawn – Erik Hofstatter
Book 20: Plain – D.T. Griffith
Book 21: Supermassive Black Mass – Matthew Davis

Book 22: Whispers Of The Sea (& Other Stories) – L. R. Bonehill
Book 23: Magic – Eric Nash
Book 24: The Plague – R.J. Meldrum
Book 25: Candy Corn – Kevin M. Folliard
Book 26: The Elixir – Lee Allen Howard
Book 27: Breaking The Habit – Yolanda Sfetsos
Book 28: Forfeit Tissue – C. C. Adams
Book 29: Crown Of Thorns – Trevor Kennedy
Book 30: The Encampment / Blood Memory – Zachary Ashford
Book 31: Dreams Of Lake Drukka / Exhumation – Mike Thorn
Book 32: Apples / Snail Trails – Russell Smeaton
Book 33: An Invitation To Darkness – Hailey Piper
Book 34: The Necessary Evils & Sick Girl – Dan Weatherer
Book 35: The Couvade – Joanna Koch
Book 36: The Camp Creeper & Other Stories – Dave Jeffery
Book 37: Flaying Sins – Ian Woodhead
Book 38: Hearts & Bones – Theresa Derwin
Book 39: The Unbeliever & The Intruder – Morgan K. Tanner
Book 40: The Coffin Walk – Richard Farren Barber
Book 41: The Straitjacket In The Woods – Kitty R. Kane
Book 42: Heart Of Stone – M. Brandon Robbins
Book 43: Bits – R.A. Busby
Book 44: Last Meal In Osaka & Other Stories – Gary Buller
Book 45: The One That Knows No Fear – Steve Stred

Book 46: The Birthday Girl & Other Stories – Christopher Beck
Book 47: Crowded House & Other Stories - S.J. Budd
Book 48: Hand To Mouth – Deborah Sheldon
Book 49: Moonlight Gunshot Mallet Flame / A Little Death – Alicia Hilton
Book 50: Dark Corners - David Charlesworth

Murder! Mystery! Mayhem!

Maggie Of My Heart – Alyson Faye
The Funeral Birds – Paula R.C. Readman
Cursed – Paul M. Feeney
The Bone Factory – Yolanda Sfetsos
Garland Cove – Deborah Sheldon
Death In The Dugout – Bruce Harris

Beats! Ballads! Blank Verse!

Book 1: Echoes From An Expired Earth – Allen Ashley
Book 2: Grave Goods – Cardinal Cox
Book 3: From Long Ago – Paul Woodward
Book 4: Laws Of Discord – William Clunie
Book 5: Fanged Dandelion – Eric LaRocca

Weird! Wonderful! Other Worlds

Book 1: The Raven King – Liz Tuckwell
Book 2: The Wired City – Yolanda Sfetsos

Horror Novels & Novellas

House Of Wrax – Raven Dane
And Blood Did Fall – Chad A. Clark

The Fallen – Anthony Watson
The Underclass – Dan Weatherer
Cheslyn Myre – Dan Weatherer
Greenbeard – John Travis
Tower Of Raven – Kevin M. Folliard
Welcome Home Natalie – Reyna Young
Little Bird – TR Hitchman
Society Place – Andrew David Barker
Axe – Terry Grimwood

The 'A QUIET APOCALYPSE' Series

A Quiet Apocalypse – Dave Jeffery
Cathedral (A Quiet Apocalypse Book 2) – Dave Jeffery
The Samaritan (A Quiet Apocalypse Book 3) – Dave Jeffery
A Silent Dystopia – Edited by D.T. Griffith

General Fiction

Joe – Terry Grimwood
Finding Jericho – Dave Jeffery

Science Fiction Collections

Vistas – Chris Kelso

Horror Fiction Collections

Distant Frequencies – Frank Duffy
Where We Live – Tim Cooke
Night Voices – Paul Edwards & Frank Duffy

Anthologies

The Darkest Battlefield – Tales Of WW1/Horror

NON-PRACTICING CULTIST
BY
SCOTT J. MOSES

A SHORT SHARP SHOCKS
BOOK!

BOOK 75

First Published 2021

For further information, please visit:
WEB: www.demainpublishing.com
TWITTER: @DemainPubUk
FACEBOOK: Demain Publishing
INSTAGRAM: demainpublishing

CONTENTS

NON-PRACTICING CULTIST

The Chevy jerks with the roughness of the Louisianan back road, the last semblance of civilization since leaving Benoit. I glance at Toby, who has one hand on the steering wheel, one around a Styrofoam cup. He grimaces and pulls the coffee from his lips, smacking them like a dog who's gotten into something spicy.

"I don't know, man," he says, smacking away. "Tastes metallic, like the pot wasn't cleaned." His eyebrows furl, and yet he brings the cup to his lips again, as if the gas station coffee will have improved between sips.

It's been nothing but swamp and gnarled cypresses for miles. We're in no-man's-land, though it's nothing I'm not used to. McKlennen was right, Louisiana and Vietnam *are* similar.

He nods to my bandaged hand. "What'd you do there?"

They're screaming.

Wailing, burning alive.

Clawing at the wooden door of the barn.

My hand hisses on the door's metal handle.

Frying like beef in a skillet.

I bring the coffee to my lips, still warm though the gas station in Benoit has to be an hour behind us.

"Burned it last week frying those bass for the Jamboree."

Toby clears his throat, tips his trucker hat with the edge of the hand gripping his coffee. "The Jamboree's always a good time. Look forward to it every year, ever since I was little...you've been at Luna's cooking, washing dishes, what...two months?"

"Just shy o' three."

"Time flies...what'd you do before all this?"

I usually keep my mouth shut, but nothing matters after tonight.

"I was in 'Nam."

He lurches back, brows raised. "Woah-ho-ho, soldier-boy. You enlist, or...?"

"Drafted in '66."

"Damn," he says, wincing at the coffee. "One of my buds was plucked by Uncle Sam a few years ago. Some luck, right? I mean, what are the odds? Three in a hundred?"

I chuckle, arm dangling from the window. "Funny how much the odds matter when it happens to you."

"I'm sure you did your fair share of killing over there." He looks through his window, the white moonlight distorted on the rippling wetlands. "Or at least, refined your taste for getting clean."

I turn to him, sip my coffee. "You sound like you enjoy it. Like it's more than ritualistic to you."

He chuckles. "You have to take pride in your work, Jim. It's what separates us from all the insects out here."

I'm back in 'Nam, staring down into the crudely dug entrance overflowing with darkness. Flashlight in one hand, revolver in the other. Breath quickening, heart slamming my chest.

"Go on, private," my CO says, as if he's cleared any of the tunnels we've come across.

I remove my shirt, and it's then the grenadier, McKlennen—on the edge of the ones huddled around the tunnel's entrance—changes his demeanor. Smiles.

"All I'm saying," Toby says, "is war is war, and you killed to survive. I know you know this. Hell, you have Croftman's brand, but what we do here is necessary too. Many cultures see sacrifice as necessary to commune with the godhead."

"The only reason I believe in God anymore is that I want someone to blame."

He chuckles. "That's rich, but you believe in what *we're* doing, right?"

"Hell, I was raised in it."

A half lie, but he runs with it.

"This shit's for real, Jim-boy. I know you were just a kid when you were with Father Croftman, but I've seen things out here in the swamp I can't explain. Gives me faith in it all."

The truck jerks again, and the rifle in the rack behind us jolts with it. A little too small for the braces holding it against the glass behind our heads. I turn to the swamp, breathe in the cool steam of the air, and take in the chorus of insects and birds sparring with the world around them.

"You know," he says, wiping the sweat from his brow. "I wasn't sure if I could trust you the night you stumbled into Luna's, half-drunk and looking for work. Hell, the way you flashed that brand like a badge should've been a red flag. But I'm glad I did, and I'm honored to know one of the First. I'm almost jealous. How'd you find us, anyway? We try to stay off the radar. Well, most of us."

"A buddy overseas turned me on to you. He saw my brand, couldn't stop staring. Found out why fairly quick. Said I'd fit right in, since I loved the heat so much. Said the food was to die for."

The light blinds me as I climb out of the tunnel, blood flecking my chest and face. Two less rounds in my revolver.

"Anyone down there, private?" my CO asks from the relative comfort of his tent.

"No, sir. Just a big fucking snake."

"And you want to keep doing this? Clearing tunnels like some rat?"

"Non gratus anus rodentum."

"'Scuse me, private?"

"Not worth a rat's ass, sir. Bit of a motto for us."

He laughs, and I wonder why we're here. Some godforsaken country, far from the Pennsylvanian forests I know. "All right, private, as you were. Get yourself some chow, there'll be more tunnels for you to skulk through soon. Whole country's riddled with them."

"Thank you, sir."

I turn and walk the dozen or so yards through the jungle to the river's edge, bend low, and cup a handful of water to my soiled face. The brush shifts behind me, and when I turn, the grenadier pushes a hanging limb ripe with jungle leaves from his path, still smiling.

He squats on the bank near me, spits into the current.

Just the two of us.

"Bet you're an orphan, huh, Bowman?"

He pulls his shirt down, dog tags dangling above a mess of scar tissue beneath his sternum. An insignia seared into his skin. A brand, like mine.

I'd buried most of what happened when I was a boy at St. Clara's Orphanage. It seemed another life, but in that moment it all came rushing back. The defenses my mind constructed, repressing the trauma, came undone. I remembered it all in the weeks that followed. How the priest who frequented St. Clara's, Father Croftman, would take a small group of us out for excursions. It was only after meeting the grenadier, Larry McKlennen, that I learned—or rather, remembered—where my nightmares of wooden water birds came from.

"And this friend," Toby says, drawing from his coffee again. "He didn't want to come with you? See our sect for himself?"

Larry McKlennen stares up at me beneath the lukewarm water of his bath in South Carolina, six months or so after our last tour in Vietnam. He'd given me what I'd wanted easy enough. Hell, he'd even shown me his mask. He was one of them, all right. The first roach I'd stomped out in a flood of many to come in this...religion.

"Has his own sect up north," I say, drumming my fingers along the metal of the passenger door.

A half-glimpsed moon keeps pace with the pickup, its glow weaving throughout the trees.

"Well, I'm glad you're here with us, Old Blood. Our sect is small, but we're doing good work."

Toby turns off the gravel road and we come to a rusted metal gate. The brakes squeal as we pull to a stop. He hops out and opens the gate, which whines on its hinges.

I check his coffee, about a third left. I stare at Toby walking back, smiling at me in the headlights, his motion still fluid, sound...oblivious. A part of me wants him to know who I am, what I've done.

He puts the Chevy in gear and we roll forward, inches from the rusted metal of the gate alongside us. A *No Trespassing* sign dangles by a lone screw as we pass. Toby leaps out again, shuts the gate behind us.

"Sorry to have kept you waiting at Luna's," he says as we crawl along the packed dirt road near the swamp's bank. "Montave wanted me to get you last, you being Father Croftman's, an' all. Not often we get newcomers, but celebrities…?"

He chuckles.

I must miss the joke.

Insects skitter atop the still water in white slivers of moonlight. Gnarled limbs hang around us like arthritic hands, drooped low from gravity's unrelenting pull.

"It's fine," I reply, and the pickup pulls into a clearing. Something long and black slips into the dark water as the headlights pass over.

A wooden pulley house rests in the glow of the headlights, the wood teetering and old, far too dilapidated for actual use. A cord or wire extends over the waters and into the black, where it's lost even in the stream of Chevy lights.

"You pull the rope a couple times and that bell up top sends for the ferry. It's not the Algiers, or anything, but it beats swimming. I'm not sure who's piloting tonight, so just tell them you're from Croftman's fold. He's a bit of a prophet around here, like Robert Plant. You like Robert Plant?"

"You're not coming?" I ask, feigning surprise.

"If you are the flock, and Montave the shepherd, think of me as the sheep dog, watchin' for threats."

Dog's blind, then.

"Thanks, Toby."

"See ya after." He leans over to rummage in the glove box, produces a flashlight, and hands it to me. "And for God's sake, watch for gators. They're big as hell out here."

He pulls his lids down, exposing the pink skin beneath.

"Their eyes shine red in the light," he says. "Not supernatural or nothin', just kinda cool."

I take the flashlight, click it on. Make my way to the bank, scanning the flat black water, the winding trees and roots springing forth from the void, clawing for air, writhing at the cosmos.

I pause and turn around, the Chevy's headlights blinding me as I squint in at Toby. He's egging me on with a hand, a *go on, go on* motion. It's silhouetted, hard to make out, though I still see him bring the coffee to his lips, see him shake his head in disgust.

I smile.

The water nibbles at the bank as I approach, and something large leaps from the expanse, plops back in with a *gulp*.

The wooden not-quite-a-dock looks worse as the flashlight passes over it, and I aim the beam up over the bronze of the rust-peppered bell.

Foster homes were mostly hell, but now and then I'd land a good one. Once, one of the good ones took me to the Liberty Bell. I barely remember their faces, or the face of their biological daughter, my would-be sister, but I remember that bell, smaller than I'd gathered from the textbooks, and cracked. There's a metaphor for life in there somewhere.

The rope, rotten and frayed, sways slightly in the breeze, an invitation.

I swing the light into the blackness surrounding the rickety dock, the planks filled with gaps and holes from neglect, no more than a foot or so above the water.

Twin red eyes glare at me from the water's surface, nostrils flared at the end of a long snout. My hand longs for the small of my back, for the pistol housed there, but I'm able to restrain myself. It's a miracle as is Toby hadn't searched me tonight. No need to give him a reason here, at the end of things.

Teeth clenched, I step toward the dock, the gator's red eyes drifting in the stillness. Her head turns with me as my boot finds the first plank.

I grasp the withered rope, flashlight trained on the red-eyed beggar. She's patiently waiting, praying I slip or creep too close to the dock's edge. The bell rings loud, like Sunday morning church bells back in Philadelphia. I pull the rope twice more, scan the flat darkness. The moon shines in frayed bits along the slow-moving current, peeking out every so often from behind the hanging vines and limbs.

I stare into those red eyes, and they mine. The burning glow leaves ember-esque trails in the slow-moving current. We stare a long while until the gator jerks to the right and opens her mouth before sinking beneath the water. I turn in the direction of the opposite bank, dark but for the moon's glow. The metal cord twitches, vibrating some feet above the water's surface. It grows rigid and twangs as the ferry comes into view. Dark, but for the moonlight's caress. Someone winds the circular pulley, feeding the cord through the mechanism, and though I can't make out much about them, their face seems wrong.

As it draws near, I aim my flashlight at the ferry's pilot. They're clad in a dark denim jacket and jeans, wearing a wooden mask crudely whittled into the face of a stork. Two dark slits for eyes, but the mask is otherwise featureless. Like a plague mask; like my childhood.

The pilot's hands fall from the wheel, and it continues its whirring as the ferry taps the dock's edge. They move to the entrance, the dark slits of their mask staring into me.

I must've been five or six when the priest took us out that first time, into the woods of rural Pennsylvania. There were four of us. The Father and his church funded the local orphanage, so no one batted an eye when he came calling. When he took us out for those nature trips. In the woods, where we donned our stork masks and were taught to sacrifice. Where we were branded. Where we—

"You deaf, or something?" the pilot asks, voice muffled beneath the wooden mask.

Their shoulders droop, and bending low, their hands heft a woodcutter's ax as they straighten again, head cocked.

"Woah, woah...I'm from Father Croftman's flock. I'm—"

The pilot laughs, bent over in a deep and breathless chuckle. They—*she*—sets the ax aside.

Amber's still laughing as she tilts the wooden mask upward, the same laugh she gives the patrons at Luna's while I stock fresh glasses at the bar. A part of me is relieved, but a larger wrenches at the sight of her.

They're not people. They can't be. They made their choices.

"God, Bowman," she says, leaning on the railing of the ferry. "You're too easy."

The memory is a torrent of electricity.

Glimpsing Croftman's sigil etched into the frame of the front door of Luna's, stumbling into the place I'd be spending most nights elbow-deep in dirty dishwater. McKlennen's map had gotten me to Benoit, the closest of two towns circled in red ink, but had given no names, dates, or specific places. Just a town in Nowhere, Louisiana, forty minutes outside of New Orleans. Worked out all right, though, and I eventually stumbled into the right place, on the third or fourth try.

Amber tended the bar, her black hair in curls, green eyes refracted in the purple light. Tattoos along her arms, all the way to the rolled-up sleeves. She'd played dumb when I showed her my brand in the mostly empty bar, a Monday, I think. Of course, she reacted how anyone would to some stranger pulling his collar down and showing their chest. Said she'd call the fucking cops if I didn't scoot, pronto. Little did I know, Toby was at the end of the bar, saw the whole thing.

Attachment is a hell of a thing, especially in my line of work, where connections are false things, made only to be severed. These people I meet, these bridges I build, only meant to be dismantled in the breath of a single night.

I climb aboard the ferry, the weight in the small of my back heavier than ever.

No guilt. They made their choices.

"Fuck you, too, Amber," I say, gripping the wooden rail as she latches the ferry's gate. She chuckles, winding the wheel, engaging the pulley. The cable whirs, the metal-on-metal buzzing like some hornet's nest aflame, and we lurch, drifting across the black.

"You're in for a treat tonight, Jim," she says over the anger of the wire. "We're humbled to have you, one of the old blood, Croftman's chosen."

And how much do you really know of the good Father, Amber? How much is tainted lies? Eroded embellishments?

"I'm not sure I believe any more...hell, I was a kid."

"Those who've lost their path find us again, one way or another. Just takes time. In the past, my faith's been rocky, too, but the things I've seen...something's happening out here, Jim. And if seeing is believing—call me a full-fledged believer."

The bastard's ragged coughs, that unsteady gait when his fits were at their worst. I think he was of a mind to live forever, drinking the blood of those later victims. May he indefinitely rot in hell.

"So this isn't an only on-holidays religion for you, is it?" I ask, a last-ditch effort to quench the guilt rising within me. "You're invested, one of the flock."

"Oh yeah, and after tonight, you'll believe too. You'll get clean and remember what being clean is to we earthly creatures. We get clean to stay sane. I need to be clean."

I swallow, turn my attention to the still water.

"How many are we tonight?"

"Usually six or seven, counting Toby and I, but Montave has something special planned."

That name.

"He called it *Fruition, Revival,*" she says, still winding the wheel. "Folks from other sects are coming to bear witness, reinvigorate, and most importantly, get clean. Times are changing, Jim. Things will be less hush-hush soon, *very soon,* and we're glad to have you."

A chill caresses my neck as the bank approaches.

The ferry taps the edge of the dock and Amber steps off, corralling the rope around a nearby post.

"Coming?" she asks, and I step onto the bank, arms and legs numb from the weight of this previous claim to Armageddon.

We walk through the swampland, the buzzing insects and cawing of the water birds ripe in the night. Her mask covers her face again, smothering her voice. Our flashlights beacons as we trudge on. Her ax rests on her shoulder, bouncing with the rhythm of her steps.

She glances back at me, eyes tracing the heron that's just leaped from a nearby limb. "Given any thought to your icon?"

"Icon?"

She taps her mask. "Your conduit, for getting clean."

How many people have seen that mask before they died? Those dark slits glaring down on them, bringing death their unfortunate way.

"When I was little, we were storks, like you."

She faces forward again. "Things have changed, Jim. Should be time enough to choose one before we're called to circle."

The forest opens to a weathered cottage. White paint-chipped columns line the porch of the one-story house. A solitary porch swing hangs still as we ascend the handful of dry wooden steps. The insects scream around us. A man in an orange hunting vest leans on the wall nearest the door, strands of hair falling from his chin in tangles beneath the wood of an elongated mask. It's different from Amber's. A fish, perhaps?

He straightens. "This him?" His voice is muffled, like he's talking through cupped hands.

Amber waves her arm in grand sarcasm. "His majesty."

The doorman crosses his arms, shifts his weight to the other leg. "All right, then..."

"What?" Amber asks.

"Strange, is all," he says, lifting the pickax from the nearby porch swing. "Montave said the Chiasson sect would bear witness, but none have come."

"You know they see this as competition," Amber says, scoffing. "They miss what it is to be divine for divinity's sake."

"Maybe..." His gaze lingers, though I only see the grooves in his mask. He moves forward. "You're the new blood, then."

"Some would say I'm *old* blood."

"So I've heard."

He lifts the sleeve of his collared shirt. A mess of tattoos embroider his arm: old badges and logos; some stick-and-poke ink, either done in prison or some kitchen on a drunken night; a crushed beer can seeping yellow liquid down to his wrist; and there, *right there,* the diagonal sharp point I bear on my chest. Mine burned in the skin, his injected in ink.

"Good to meet—"

"We'll handle formalities after the gathering," he says. He opens the door, steps inside. "Time's a-wasting."

We enter a mostly vacant space. Two worn, gray-cushioned chairs sit in the room's corner, and a formation of unlit candles are splayed on the mantle above a dormant hearth. The dust in the air is palpable. An ancient shotgun lies across two protruding pieces of wood above the hearth. The space between the weapon and the mantle lush with thick cobwebs. Hell, the entire room is nothing more than wood, webs, and dust. Amber extinguishes the beam of her flashlight, leaves it lens-down on the mantle. She looks to me and I set mine next to hers.

We continue down the hall at the doorman's hurried pace, the rooms along the walls receiving no more than cursory glances. Most seem vacant, from what I can tell in the seconds I have to examine them. This house is just that, housing something greater.

We enter a kitchen. The sink is empty, rust creeping in at the corners. Doors hang loose or are missing entirely from the L-shaped cabinets above the sink and counter. Amber grasps a metal rung built into the wall beneath a pair of heavily dusted pictures. She hefts the rung and the wall gives way, leaving the open section to rest against the atrophying counter.

Cooler air pools from the secret compartment's mouth, a contrast from the rampant humidity of the bayou. The doorman steps inside first, descending the stairs into utter darkness.

My heart slams in my chest. The dark pit an unholy void, an entrance to nothing and everything. My mind relays images of Vietnam and Laos and all those jungle-ridden countries whose depths I've survived, gasping for breath as my head breaks the surface, eyes squinting from the blinding sun, flashlight and revolver slick in my trembling hands.

I grip the counter. The kitchen swaying like some ship on rough seas.

"You all right?" Amber asks, mask tilted upward, green eyes on mine.

I find my breath and the jungle dissipates. The feeling creeps back into my hands, arms, and chest, a million needles gnawing the flesh in a slow crawl.

I release my white-knuckled grip of the counter. "I'm good..."

The counter's surface brighter where my tightened fingers dispersed the grime.

"You sure?" She takes a step forward. "Claustrophobic or something?"

"I'm fine. Let's go."

"All right," she says, mask slipping down over her face again. A reminder of what she really is, what they all are.

What's one more tunnel?

As I descend the last step, my boots meet with the dilapidated floor of what might've been a cellar, though I've yet to see a cellar in all of Louisiana; ground's too susceptible to water out here. Wooden pillars of the underhouse protrude up into the floor above. It seems we entered not from the first floor, but the second, and we're now on what was originally the ground floor. The space seems vacant in the dark, and it's only when Amber is swallowed up by the adjacent wall that my eyes adjust. Orange lights flicker via candlelight in the narrow hall, and Amber looks over her shoulder. She waves me over and I follow, running my hand along the decrepit walls, fingers every so often grazing more of the wooden pillars lining the unfinished floor.

"How far does it go?" I ask, but she slices the air in the way she does when flirting with a generous tipper.

I chuckle.

I like Amber, I do. Took her awhile to open up to me, but I feel like we could—

My stomach pangs, the realization acidic.

Amber isn't that snarky bartender from Luna's. That's a persona, a mask she dons to make ends meet.

I round the bend, and Amber stands before a pair of wooden double doors. She adjusts her mask, the eyes of the stork ever watchful.

How much do you really see, Amber?

She motions to the doors behind her. "Find your face, then follow the hall farther up. Immerse yourself in your choice, it'll help with what happens next."

I hardly catch what she says as my hands grow numb.

She knows. God, she knows.

Chiasson was easier.

She knows.

Toby knows.

They're onto me, they're—

"Jim?" she asks, fingers drumming her arm.

I manage a nod. "Won't be long."

She smiles beneath her mask, I can tell.

"Take your time."

She reaches up, grips my arm tight, and walks off, leaving me alone before the double doors.

The wood whines as I push through the doors and enter the small room. A man, gray in his beard and bald, wearing a cut-off leather vest, stares at me and then back at the wall of faces before us.

A plethora of wooden masks hang from railroad stakes driven into wooden pillars. Storks, alligators, a serpent, a fish, a snapping turtle, a dog or two, what might be a cat or fox, all crudely carved. I imagine a centuries-old crone in a marshland shanty, whittling with rusted cutlery and cackling, hands covered in blood.

I glance at the biker, who lifts the largest mask from one of the spikes. A snapping turtle. I know from the broad, diamond-shaped beak.

Hometown hero of the ol' south.

He tries on the mask, rolls his shoulders, and with a turn, hefts the pickax I'd missed, closing the door behind him.

I breathe in the captive must of the windowless room. Two candles flicker on either side of the table beneath the masks impaled to the board like insects in a school science project.

I look over my shoulder, pause, and remove the pistol stowed in the small of my back.

I drop the mag, check its contents, pull the slide back. A brass-encased friend winks at me as I release the mechanism. I flick the safety off and return it to the holster. No one's frisked me, not in Chiasson either. That was worse than expected, but I lucked out.

They were a sect of four, and there'd been plenty of gasoline.

They're crying, burning alive in that ragged barn where they performed their ritual.

Tears burn my eyes from the other side of the door, and for a moment, an instant, I grip the metal of the door's handle.

It's molten hot and I yank it back, gritting my teeth. As if the door and that night say in one voice, "No take-backs."

Footsteps beyond the doors stop me dead. I look over the masks and reach my hand out to one, a wolf or dog, some lanky thing, a fox? I fit the mask over my eyes, and the candlelight grows instead of dimming, the mask focusing the light somehow. The visibility greater than expected despite the small circular eyeholes.

As I fasten the mask, the doors open behind me.

"You good?" Amber asks, cocking her stork head.

My exhales echo throughout the heavy wood. The heat of my own breath crawls over my face.

"Acclimating."

She nods, as if this means anything at all, and holds a door for me. I roll my neck, preparing for another tunnel. Another enemy buried beneath the rubble of it all.

Tunnel Rat then, Tunnel Rat now.

We follow the corridor to another set of doors, and Amber pauses, looks back at me. "Don't get starstruck."

Before I can ask, she pushes them open and the pale moonlight rolls over us.

The sounds of the insects return as we step out into the swampland. Three figures stand before a makeshift altar, a gargantuan sheet draped over a mound of what looks to be rubble arranged in human form.

I step forward, eye them each in turn.

Just like Chiasson.

They regard me, and I count the doorman and snapping turtle among them. A figure emerges from behind the altar. He's wearing a gray suit, elbows and knees muddy from kneeling where the water meets the earth.

"Old Blood," he says, and smiles at his congregation. "Everyone, we have with us an *original*. One of Croftman's own flock."

The three nod in my direction, all in masks, before returning to the one behind the altar. The bank is lined with makeshift torches planted in the soil; a half moon of miniature flames alive in the night. A thick mess of limbs and vines hang all around us, as if in wait.

He flashes his pearly whites—I know this man. I've seen him on the television mounted in the corner of the bar every day for the last three months.

Holy shit.

Bill Montave, of the *Channel 31* news, approaches me. Smiling as if he's just leaped in front of the green screen to give the afternoon weather report.

"My, oh my, it's an honor to have you here with us, Old Blood."

I struggle for words.

He notices, chuckles. "Can't help what we do in the day now, can we? You know as well as I that those who wish to be cleansed come from all circles."

I nod, shaking his hand. I've done that often, given my hand to those unworthy of it. But I'll have the last laugh tonight. One night of many to come in this game I've grown fond of.

"Honored, Mr Montave." Our hands clench. He gives me a toothy, *Back to you, Jane,* smile before turning around, making his way to the altar again. Something large plunges beneath the flat water behind him, and some bird flies overhead, caw-caw-cawing.

He stands behind the altar now, hands placed on the rickety wood beneath the hulking thing atop it. "Tonight, we raise one of our own in Father Croftman's name. It is a precious gift, when you are of the flock, to never die."

Montave flashes that 90210 smile of his, teeth shimmering in the moonlight.

"Friends, brethren, tonight is a night we've waited for. We've toiled, bled for this. And I want you to know your sacrifice isn't in vain. Walter Clemenceau was our brother, *still* is our brother, and we take care of our own. But a soul cannot be hefted from the expanse without equal exchange, without payment in blood. Tonight is about more than satiating our…" He pauses, and the corners of his lips curl, "…more *primal* appetites. This is about bending the nature of what we've done over the last decade to our will. Tonight is about fruition."

Where a live audience would normally applaud, the swamp is still.

Amber nudges my arm.

I'm unaware of how long she's been there.

Montave lifts his hands as if blessing a meal, and without a sound the collective forms a line. A rust-laden basin sits atop a roaring fire, its innards black, bubbling. The first of us, the snapping turtle in cut-off denim sleeves, removes his mask and dips it into the goop. He fastens it to his face, inhaling like he's broken the water's surface seconds before drowning, and steps aside. The tattooed doorman does the same.

A woman ahead of me follows suit, filing to the left after snorting the concoction. I walk to the basin's edge, examine its contents. A black muck, like tar, rests thick and semi-solid. Bubbles exhale at its surface.

I don't remember this.

"Go on, Jim," Amber says behind me, voice muffled and thick from the wood of her icon.

I remove my mask and submerge it into the dark gunk. The smell is putrid, like melted rubber, the palpable afterburn lingering on the swamp air. I wriggle my nose and pause before placing the mask to my face.

Montave's hands are clasped, and he watches me with a smile. Wafting the stench to his nostrils, he takes a deep breath, instructs me to do the same.

I inhale the poison and my lungs roar with flame. I figure if it isn't Agent Orange that gets me later in life, it'll be this, but also assume this is like teens passing a bowl: you're one of us, or a snitch.

I step aside as Amber removes her mask, dipping it into the warmed goop ripe with herbs and plants. She files off to the right and stands across from me. The two of us now closest to Montave and whatever the white sheet conceals.

"Breeeeathe..." he says, motioning with his hands like some instructional video. "Breeeathe..."

I blink hard as the once-still waters behind Montave and the altar churn with fury. My throat is raw, dry...like I've swallowed a carton of cigarettes, package and all.

I cough, wretched and ragged, and the others' heads sway like the leaves on the limbs all around us. Stuttering like the flashes of a camera, shuttering in stop-motion.

A hand finds my shoulder and I gasp. Montave stands over me, the long mask of what looks to be a catfish over his face. The mask stretches into his skin, the wood clawing for ground beneath the flesh, blood seeping out from where the wood meets humanity.

"Let it take you, Old Blood. The first time is...a necessary experience."

His voice is deep, not that white-toothed southern accent heard minutes before. The black eyes of his mask, no, *his face*, blink, now fully sealed to his skin. My breath halts as the mask compresses, constricting my neck, and as my eyes grow tight, fur grows from the pores of my face. A cold, wet nose and mouth lined with smooth, sharp teeth.

"The coyote has taken to you," he says, liquid dripping down the barbs protruding from his gaping fish lips. Black eyes bulge on either side of his head. I can hardly breathe, but manage to form words with a longer tongue than usual.

"What...is this?"

Montave looks into me with those dead black eyes, torches gleaming in the darkness behind him. "See to the stock, Old Blood. Bring forth the means to pluck Clemenceau from the expanse."

He looks behind me, and a hulk steps forward. It's hunched, broad-shouldered, and the weight of its step sends the earth trembling. The turtle rears its beaked head toward Montave and nods, opening its triangular mouth. It looks to me before making its way to the door.

Montave extends a hand and I follow the turtle back to the house, built into what must be the highest point of the island. An incline of grass, rock, and trees line either side of the decrepit structure. My eyes catch the skeletal bird woman's smile, though the beak left ajar could mean anything.

Humanoids loom around me, and I only recognize them for their clothes. A pale fish, smaller than Montave, bearing black stripes along his cheeks, yellow eyes on either side of his face, opens a door for us as we walk through. A lanky squirrel says something I miss as it closes behind us.

Candles along the planked walls light our way as I follow the turtle. He looks over his shoulder, grunting as drool falls from his beak, and we turn right where the hall forks. We come to a dead end, and he pulls on the rusted knob of the plank door which opens to a room no larger than a closet.

The turtle says something, sets his pickax beside him, and bends low. Someone screams and my coyote ears perk up. The voice of a woman and rattling chains echo from the earthen cell. The turtle shifts to the side.

I see her.

She's dressed in the dusted navy blue diner uniform she was last seen in, brown hair matted in knots.

Wendy Carrington.

She looks at me and then the turtle, her whimpers give way to sobs. The turtle gropes for the pickax, his eyes still on Wendy. I give it to him, arms trembling from the recoil as it sinks into his back.

Wendy screams and shoves by us. I lick my lips with my newfound tongue, taste turtle blood for the first time, fur bristling on the back of my head beneath pointed ears. I rip the ax from the motionless monster, whose blood coats the floor of the small cell. I turn, but Wendy's gone like the devil's come to collect, her screams my only sense of her whereabouts.

I round the corner where the hall forks and see her burst through the wooden doors to the ceremony outside. She stops, screams. The striped bass's mouth opens, the squirrel grinds her flattened teeth. Wendy pivots and slips in the slick soil but finds traction and blows by me. Amber's thin stork feathers ruffle as she screams, gives chase. She slams into me and my head hammers the wall, sending bursts of light exploding behind my eyes. Through the white-static barrage in my brain, I glimpse them disappearing around the corner, where the hall bends left from the mask room's entrance, the ax lost from the impact. The striped bass stares at me, and a long line of drool descends to the dirt beneath him.

I bare my fangs and pull the M1911 from the small of my back. An array of colors burst through the back of his skull with the echo of the fired round.

The squirrel lunges, swings her shovel at my head. I duck, the debris of the wall trickling into the fur behind my ears. I pivot and launch three more rounds in a frenzy, dust and dirt exploding, punching holes in the nearby wall. She hefts the shovel, takes a step forward, and groans, holding her reddening gut. When I think she'll collapse, she growls, steps forward again, but Montave's voice staves her. She whips her head back and retreats to the altar.

I shake the remaining stars from my vision and lift my pistol—I'm on my back, white-hot pain erupting in my skull. I shake my head, see two clenched hands bearing down on me, and roll on the uneven floor, just avoiding them. The turtle trembles on its feet, crying tears of green, its breath ragged.

How the hell...?

Wheezing, he places himself between me and the open doors leading to the ritual.

He stumbles, then charges, and I plant my back on the wall. He sprawls to the floor. I bend, swipe up the pistol, and unleash the rest of the clip into his back. Voices rise behind me. The corpse of the striped bass is on the altar now, Montave and the squirrel's hands are lifted, both speaking a guttural language. I discard the pistol and pull the Saturday night special from my ankle. A scream shakes the walls of the house around me.

ShitShitSHIT.

Reluctantly, I turn, follow the cry.

There's only one way off this island.

I sprint through the hallway, stealing a final glance behind me before banking left at the mask room.

Outside, the figure beneath the white sheet sits upright.

***

Another scream tunnels toward me as I stumble in the low-lit darkness, my coyote nose pulling in the humid scent of damp soil. My vision trembles.

I pull myself together, retracing my steps, and the space gives way to the not-quite-a-cellar. Wendy is scrambling on all fours to a corner of the room, the steps leading up to the kitchen just beyond reach. The stork steps around on stilted legs, drool lining the rim of her long beak. The fur on my neck rises, and I growl words with my new, elongated tongue.

"Amber," I say, miniature pistol extended. "Don't. Please...don't."

The stork looks back at me and lifts the ax over Wendy. Feathers flushed, spread in anger.

I lift the pistol, praying to God and whatever else the piece of shit won't fail, remembering the words of the sleazy dealer who sold it to me in South Carolina.

"They're made cheap, but concealable. Likely to jam or crumble to nothing in your hand."

I let loose three rounds and Amber groans, falling to her knees. Wendy curls in on herself behind the stairs. I steady myself with the wall and corral my coyote tongue, coaxing it to form words.

"Wendy, we're getting out. I'm a friend. I'm—"

She looks confused as the malformed words leave my snout.

I yawn, stretching my animal tongue into submission, try again. "A ferry...through the front door a ways."

I step forward, she recoils.

"I'm a friend. Wait for me."

She pauses, devoid of response, and leaps up the stairs like some startled cat.

I circle the stairs, pistol extended pointed at Amber, who lies in a growing pool at their base.

She's muttering something...beak opening and closing in rhythm with her breathing. I bend low, coyote ears drooped as I stare into her stork eyes. She's still in there, somewhere.

"Need cleeeean...cleeeean," she says, her breath ragged and wheezing from what's likely a pierced lung.

I gag, lick my coyote lips.

"There's a difference between wanting and needing something," I say, leaning closer. Sniffing with my coyote nose. "Which is it, Amber?"

Father Croftman runs the blood of our first sacrifice along the brows of our masks. Me and two other orphans, a brother and sister, the first in this game of murder.

"You're clean now, child. God requires blood sacrifice, like the Israelites before us. Blood is the standard payment for sin, the weight in holy gold to the Father."

The victim, an old man Croftman found only hell knows where, lay mangled from where the Father had broken his legs with the baseball bat. He'd given us children garden spades and shears. Told us to go to work, and so we did. He was an adult, and adults knew best.

"Cleeeeean...cleeeeean," she says again, her arm swiping the floor for the ax beyond reach. Her wheezing is worse, now accompanied by a bubbling with each inhale.

"This isn't how you get clean, Amber. Never was..."

A groan rises from behind me, and it's then I notice how dark the room is.

I rise, turn, and bare my coyote teeth.

A behemoth blocks the mouth of the hall. His skin is gray, ripe with boils and lacerations. One side of his face is slack, like a stroke-victim, the other is furled, angry. His black suit is caked in dust and grime—perhaps the suit he was buried in.

It's the chemicals, just the chemicals...

The hulk towers over me, but is otherwise still. I point my sidearm in his direction, breath held. I'll be lucky if the .22s even break skin.

"Mr Bowman," Montave calls from deep in the hallway. "Mr Clemenceau."

The thing jerks at his name, like hearing it is the pull-start to the engine that is his brain.

"You've gone astray, Old Blood. How could you betray your own ilk?"

I back toward the stairs, eyes still on Clemenceau, whose shoulders rise with every step.

Montave peaks out from behind Clemenceau, who grits his dead teeth at me, yellowed and stained with the blood of the striped bass's sacrifice.

"Keep silent, then," Montave says, catfish barbs twinging like plucked strings. Clemenceau steps toward me and the earth trembles. He rears his head in a long groan peppered with croaks.

I empty the pistol and Clemenceau shields his face, swatting at what may as well be mosquitoes.

The steps whine with the weight of my boots. I explode into the kitchen and sprint down the hall to the main room. The front door's ajar, the black water outside glistening in the moonlight.

I stop at the door, remember the heirloom above the mantle.

I lift the shotgun from its place, the cobwebs giving way as I break it open, revealing two rusted shells inside. Running my hand along the mantle, another falls to the floor. The room is ripe with dust, and I sneeze, shaking out my fur before sneezing again.

Wriggling my nose, I lock in the double-barrel and sprint back down the hall to the kitchen. Clemenceau groans, struggling to squeeze himself through the door's opening. A long arm gropes at the sink for leverage.

I lift the shotgun, grit my coyote teeth, and pull the first trigger.

Click. Nothing.

ShitSHIT.

The hands retreat then grasp either side of the doorframe, and Clemenceau pulls himself in, his head, neck, and shoulders tearing out in unholy birth. I lift the shotgun—

Please.

—and pull the second trigger.

The wall explodes and Clemenceau groans, his buckshot-shredded hand flailing for purchase as he collapses to the first floor, shaking the bones of the house.

I break the weapon, eject the empty shell.

Dropping the other, I pull the hammer back and another barrage severs the steps bridging the two floors. The shotgun falls to the floor and my coyote ears brush the underside of the doorway.

I run through an ocean of cypresses, coyote tongue dangling, the scents and sounds of the swamp alive, welcoming. The insects cry as I reach the ferry docked at the pier. Wendy's curled inside, knees in her hands, and hardly moves at my approach. I hop on, pull the rope from the nearby post, find the wheel Amber turned on the voyage over, and propel us across the expanse.

My arms burn.

I wind for an eternity as the ferry drifts to the other side of the bank, my coyote tongue drooped and panting in the heat. The headlights of Toby's Chevy creep through the fog in luminescence.

The ferry thumps the edge of the dock, rocking slowly in the still black water. Wendy's looking at me, analyzing.

"Wendy Carrington, right?" I say. "Elburn, Louisiana?"

She nods, shivering despite the heat.

"I'm taking you home, back to Elburn."

"You're not one of them, are you?"

"No. No, I'm not."

I extend my hand, and she takes it. She can't be more than twenty. The brown hair matted to one side of her face is covered in dirt and grime.

We step off the ferry, feet hitting the bank above the dock where water meets land.

I look to the truck and back to Wendy, who squints in the glare of the headlights, smiling up at me.

Wendy's on her back before the rifle's cry reaches the trees. The chest of her uniform grows crimson in the Chevy's lights. She convulses, eyes wide.

I run to a nearby cypress, place my back against the bark.

NoNO.

Wood explodes from the trunk of the tree, inches above my head.

Toby should be dead. All that arsenic would've killed a bull.

I wait, eyes on Wendy, now motionless on the bank.

Forgive me.

I rest my head against the trunk, figure he's walking 'round to put a bullet in me.

My vision blurs as I stare out over the stillness. The white light of the moon shimmering in lines atop the black.

Not a horrible way to die.

Some people get cancer.

Some are imprisoned in nursing homes, unvisited the last years of their lives.

I peek around the splintered trunk, stare up at the Chevy. A million insects swarm the glow of the headlights. No sign of Toby.

I'm patient, but death's sure taking its time.

I rise with a groan and pain spreads through my veins. I stumble up the bank, gritting my coyote teeth, wincing with each step and slipping in the mud before reaching the truck. The driver's door is open, Toby Craw and his hunting rifle splayed beneath it. He smells of shit, piss, and vomit. A generous amount of drool lines his newly dead lips.

Here lies Toby Craw, dead too late.

I pull myself into the truck and sigh as my head finds the headrest, panting with my coyote tongue. The putrid stench of the sect's chemical still ripe in my nose, my lungs.

An unholy roar echoes across the still waters, lifts my gaze to the opposite bank. I slide out from the truck, landing on Toby's corpse, and pull the rifle from his hand. Wincing, I rise and level the weapon in the groove where the door meets the rest of the truck. I pull back the bolt, ejecting the empty brass, and slam it forward, wrap the rifle strap around my arm.

I'm in the jungle again.

My vision magnifies through the rifle's scope, and breath held, I scan the stillness until...

...Clemenceau.

He's swimming, walking, or both, lifting his head high where the water climbs to his throat. Montave is on Clemenceau's shoulders, scaly fish skin gleaming in the moonlight. The two rise as they near the bank, the surface of the water draining to Clemenceau's chest, then stomach.

I pull the trigger and Clemenceau lurches back, head whipping up in the headlights of Toby's truck. He bares his dead man's teeth at me.

Montave screams a muffled order, and I adjust the rifle and fire. He jerks back but manages to remain on Clemenceau's shoulders—then the cavalry arrives. I'd seen her red eyes creeping in behind them, and Montave screams as she pulls him in.

Can't have me, doll, but don't say I never got you anything.

Montave wails as the gator pulls him into the darkness. Clemenceau slams both fists into the water, barely keeping himself above the surface. I eject the round, bring my eye to the scope again, and fire another at the dead man. His neck jolts back and he collapses into the group of crimson eyes all around him. They close in and he sinks beneath the black. I watch the water through the scope a while. Nothing resurfaces.

My eyes find Wendy Carrington, still splayed on the bank, innocent to all of this but a victim nonetheless.

I resign that I'll bury her, let her folks know what happened. The rifle tips over the door to the ground and I stumble into the driver's seat, head and eyes heavy.

So heavy.

Darkness becomes me.

***

"Hard, Jim. With purpose."

My wide-eyed gaze meets the Father's own. We're in the woods of rural Pennsylvania, me and two other orphans, chosen for hell knows why. "Child or no, the business of making yourself clean is serious."

I nod, bite my lip, and focus on the bound man. Lanky, dirty...sack over his face, unclean. He's whimpering, and as he inhales I bring the garden spade down on his head. He's still after that, and without a word, the other children, a girl and boy, and Croftman himself place their hands on my head and shoulders.

"There, there, Jim-boy. Don't cry. Doesn't that feel nice? Getting clean?"

"Private Bowman," my CO says, uniform unbuttoned, blood-stained tank top beneath. "Don't that feel nice? Getting clean?"

His jaw hangs from his face, the teeth a necklace of pearls disappearing into the darkness of his twitching throat.

McKlennen pokes up from one of the VC tunnels, the entrance alive with flame. He's laughing, though entirely engulfed, and two deep holes that once were eyes stare into me.

"Bet you're an orphan, huh, Bowman?"

My mouth is sewn shut, and I turn to the stork pecking at the embroidered name on my uniform. It draws back, tilts its head.

"I need this, Jim," Amber says, her movements stilted and stuttering as she nuzzles her beak along the skin of my neck.

Wendy Carrington looks up from the bank, shrugs. "You tried."

***

Hot breath on my face, and my eyes open to dawn overflowing in waves of orange.

Squinting, I sit up with a groan, one leg draped over the passenger seat and shifter of Toby's truck. Birds sing off time from one another.

My head throbs and I lift the mask from my face, assaulted with the coming dawn. My back cracks as I right myself. Sitting up in the driver's seat, I draw in the sticky air.

Something stirs in my periphery, and I lurch back at the alligator's muzzle creeping in through the open door. She looks up at me, mouth opening over the corpse of Toby Craw, who she's taken exploratory chomps into. I lift my hand, wave.

She stares, mouth gaping, her eyes spelling death for any man who touches her. A lady should dine in peace.

My hands grip the wheel, and I squint at the shimmered orange reflected on the water.

Wendy's gone. No burying her now...hell, could I even reach her family if I tried? Four months is a long time without your little girl...but people are resourceful. Maybe they rationalize that *not knowing* what happened to their daughter is better—and here some unknown marches up to their door and says their little girl was shot, then eaten. Have a nice one.

I lay my head on the worn headrest. McKlennen's map marked two towns, Chiasson and Benoit. Now, well...

What now?

With a sigh, I lean over the shifter and click the button on the glove box, which vomits an array of papers, cigarette packaging, and a road map. I raise a brow and lift it to my presumably bloodshot eyes. The map boasts a plethora of pen-scribbled stars atop the printed names of towns spreading throughout the state, a few as far as Mississippi and Texas.

I squint hard and count to three, wanting to make sure this isn't some hallucination. A trick of the eye or inebriated mind. I survey the map again. If anything, there are more than before. Perhaps inked in while my eyes were closed.

Chiasson, Benoit...two of dozens—maybe hundreds. Really is hopeless, then.

My mistress hisses and turns, mouth ajar, before chomping down on Toby's corpse and yanking him to the water's edge. Grimacing, my eyes flick to the rearview mirror, reflection alive with flashing reds and blues.

With a groan, I straighten in the driver's seat, glimpsing Toby's shirt, jeans, then boots slink under the water, as if crawling in himself.

Two officers exit the car, leaving their respective doors ajar. One hefts a shotgun, the other a flashlight and pistol.

The beam of the flashlight crawls up the still-open driver's door and stops on the steering wheel, resting on me.

"Hands on the dash, now," the officer says, rounding the open door, pistol trained on me from outside the truck.

I comply, clenching my eyes in the white-hot light.

"Out of the vehicle. Don't make me ask twice."

I nod and slink out of the truck like syrup from a basin.

"Hands where I can see them."

I lift them, and my muscles scream with the night's labor. I scan the swamp for some semblance of what happened here.

"Listen," I say, turning to the light again. "That missing girl, Wendy Carrington, she's in the water there. There's a house across—"

"Step out where I can see you," he says. The orange sun glints off the dark lenses of his aviators.

I do so, and in the beam of his flashlight realize I'm stained with blood.

He's stern, face dusted in five o'clock shadow. If the blood fazes him, he doesn't let on, and he nudges the air with his pistol. "Over there, that mess of trees. Sit."

Though my body pangs, my mind whispers one word—

Run.

"Don't do anything stupid," he says behind me. I limp over to the intermingling trees, slump at their feet. The officer looks down on me, sighs, and slides the pistol into its holster.

The second officer, her blonde hair in a taut ponytail and wearing dark aviators, rounds the truck, wood-gripped shotgun in one hand, coyote mask in the other.

She tosses it at my feet. "The hell is this?"

"This is gonna sound—"

"Been in Chiasson lately?" the male interrupts, and it's then I see the side of the cruiser: **Chiasson Police.**

My eyes meet his. "Never."

He chuckles and looks to his partner, who approaches me. She crouches, her face inches from mine. My image reflected in the polarized lenses. She points at my hand.

"How'd you do that?"

"I'm a cook. Burned it on the line."

She smiles, tilts her head at her partner.

The male's shoulders shake, and he lifts a hand to the swamp. "Toby Craw may have fallen for that, but we know better."

The woman shakes her head, sighs. "We found the barn, or what was left of it. You burned them alive. Learn that in 'Nam?"

I sit forward. "I don't know what you're talking about."

She leans in, removes her aviators. "We found Larry McKlennen face-up in his tub, eyes on God, pondering the mistakes of his life." She leans closer still. "His map was gone, so we figured whoever killed him would be in Louisiana. For being in 'Nam, you sure were easy to track."

"Who are you people? Sure as hell aren't cops."

She smirks, looks to her partner. "Wow, Joel, a real bona fide genius."

Joel smiles. "He doesn't remember, Mary. He was young, adopted before—"

He stops and turns to the police cruiser a few yards from us, beneath the shelter of coagulated, hanging limbs. Mary rises, steps toward him. I listen, but only hear the buzzing of insects stirring as an orange sun rises in the purple expanse. Then...a whisper, barely audible atop the swamp's waking song.

I crane my head, stomach curling.

"Go, *go,*" Mary says, and Joel hurries to the flashing reds and blues.

She plucks up the coyote mask, examines it.

"Pretenders," she says, tossing it aside. "You were meant for more."

Joel opens the rear door of the cruiser, and a lanky figure steps out. He brushes off his peacoat, rolls his neck back and forth. He's tall, *too tall*, and seems to grow higher as he groans and stretches out. He's pale white, skeleton thin.

Joel says something and lifts his hand, but the figure pins him to the trunk. The reds and blues wash along the tall one's face. His mouth is ajar, and loose strands of white hair fall down his shoulders. He releases Joel, who scampers to the passenger door, rummaging inside the vehicle. The figure cocks his head, closes the distance between us in too few steps. I'm eclipsed in his shadow, this manufactured nightfall.

His skin is gray, and black holes burrow into his skull where eyes should be.

It's the chemicals, just the chemicals.

He looms over me and extends a long, gray hand with gnarled fingers.

"You've been busy, boy..." he says, utterly still but for the whispers, those black voids burning through me.

I'm shaking, muscles tensed, though my hands are numb, head is spinning. "No...you're..."

He straightens, and his shoulders shake. A hissing laugh like static flows throughout the swamp's entirety.

Joel hands Mary something I can't quite see and she slips it over her face. They step to the tall one's side, aviators traded for masks I've not seen in decades. They stare at me through dark slits above long beaks.

The tall one's hand shoots to my throat, pinning me to the knotted bark.

My lungs wrench for oxygen, blood pools in my head. A hissing sound cuts through my blurred vision, brings him into focus. My body a thousand useless pounds.

"Who *am* I...?"

I'm gagging, pulling at the stone hand around my throat.

I'm a boy.

In St. Clara's.

Looking up at a man whose smile is as big as the gray sky outside the orphanage.

He clasps my cheek, and a child smiles.

"Fa...Father—"

I plummet to the ground, gasp for air, curling into a ball as my vision seeps back. His stench is unbearable, like the goop from Montave's ritual, yet...familiar. That sugar-sweet stench I can't seem to shake—death.

"You're tainted," Father Croftman says, and bending at an unholy angle, he lifts the coyote mask from the grass. The blood of last night flecked across its snout.

Mary crouches, leaning on her shotgun. Stork mask muffling her voice, she says, "You killed McKlennen, didn't you?"

The four of us draining the blood of the bound man into plastic milk jugs.

Walking out of the woods together, a family. Father Croftman, Joel, Mary, and me.

"No use denying it," Joel says, voice muffled from the thick wood of his mask. "Hell, we were on our way to do the same, but you beat us there. McKlennen came later, but he never replaced you. He got a big head, stemmed these false sects along the coast to the gulf."

Croftman lifts me like I'm nothing, pulls me close. My feet kick, as if treading bottomless water.

"Imitations," Croftman whispers, his stench acidic. "Sinful excuses for what we alone know. They blaspheme in their attempts at divinity. Squabbling among one another, devoid of truth."

He straightens, and the vertebrae of his spine crack like stones.

"I am perfection. I am eternal...and I stamp out those who water down my practice."

I'm a child in his grasp.

"You've lost your way," he says, face inching closer. "Though I will accept the sacrifice of the heretic, McKlennen...if you claim responsibility."

His gaze eviscerates me.

I want to scream, cry like the boy I was—still am.

Remembering the commandments learned in St. Clara's.

The sting of the ruler's strike on my hand.

Thou shalt not bear false witness against thy neighbor.

Honor thy father and mother.

I look to the only father I've ever known, tears filling my eyes.

"I…I killed him, I—"

My vision goes white, and blood trickles down the back of my head. I writhe in the dead man's iron hands.

Gagging, I claw at my throat. The curtains of my peripheral vision narrowing.

"Forgotten the words, boy?"

"Bless me, Father for I have sinned…"

Our cheeks brush, and he whispers to me, as he did in life.

"What are your sins, my son?"

BIOGRAPHY

Scott J. Moses is the author of *Non-Practicing Cultist* (Demain Publishing) and *Hunger Pangs* (independently published). A member of the Horror Writers Association, his work has appeared in Paranormal Contact (Cemetery Gates Media), Diabolica Americana (Keith Anthony Baird), Planet Scumm, and elsewhere. He also edited *What One Wouldn't Do: An Anthology on the Lengths One Might Go To*. You can find him on Twitter @scottj_moses or at www.scottjmoses.com

ADRIAN BALDWIN (COVER ARTIST)

Adrian is a Mancunian now living and working in Wales. Back in the 1990s, he wrote for various TV shows/personalities: Smith & Jones, Clive Anderson, Brian Conley, Paul McKenna, Hale & Pace, Rory Bremner (and a few others). Wooo, get him! Since then, he has written three screenplays—one of which received generous financial backing from the Film Agency for Wales. Then along came the global recession which kicked the UK Film industry in the nuts. What a bummer! Not to be outdone, he turned to novel writing—which had always been his real dream—and, in particular, a genre he feels is often overlooked; a genre he has always been a fan of: Dark Comedy (sometimes referred to as Horror's weird cousin). *Barnacle Brat* (a dark comedy for grown-ups), his first novel won Indie Novel of the Year 2016 award; his second novel *Stanley Mccloud Must Die!* (more dark comedy for grown-ups) published in 2016 and his third: *The Snowman And The Scarecrow* (another dark comedy for grown-ups) published in 2018. Adrian Baldwin has also written and published a number of dark comedy short stories. He designs book covers too—not just for his own books but for a growing number of publishers. For more information on the award-winning author, check out:

https://adrianbaldwin.info/

DEMAIN PUBLISHING

To keep up to-date on all news DEMAIN (including future submission calls and releases) you can follow us in a number of ways:

BLOG:
www.demainpublishingblog.weebly.com

TWITTER:
@DemainPubUk

FACEBOOK PAGE:
Demain Publishing

INSTAGRAM:
demainpublishing

www.ingramcontent.com/pod-product-compliance
Ingram Content Group UK Ltd.
Pitfield, Milton Keynes, MK11 3LW, UK
UKHW041844200726
13854UKWH00005BA/2070

9 798781 240104